Nikola Tesla Lights the World

Fiona Jacobson

INFOMAX COMMON CORE READERS

Rosen Classroom™

New York

Published in 2014 by The Rosen Publishing Group, Inc.
29 East 21st Street, New York, NY 10010

Book Design: Jon D'Rozario

Photo Credits: Cover (Tesla) Photo Researchers/Photo Researchers/Getty Images; cover (lightning) Martin Capek/Shutterstock.com; cover (background) Irina_QQQ/Shutterstock.com; pp. 3, 4, 6, 8, 10, 12, 14, 16, 18, 20, 22, 23, 24 (background) voylodyon/Shutterstock.com; pp. 5, 22 (Tesla) Georgios Kollidas/Shutterstock.com; p. 7 SuperStock/SuperStock/Getty Images; p. 9 Mondadori/Mondadori/Getty Images; p. 11 (main) iStockphoto/Thinkstock.com; p. 11 (inset) Nikola Bilic/Shutterstock.com; pp. 13, 22 (Tesla coil) Arthur S. Aubry/Photodisc/Getty Images; p. 15 Olga Lyubkina/Shutterstock.com; p. 17 Hulton Archive/Archive Photos/Getty Images; p. 19 Mesut Dogan/Shutterstock.com; p. 21 Joseph Moran/Shutterstock.com; p. 22 (city) elwynn/Shutterstock.com; p. 22 (car) stephenkirsh/Shutterstock.com; p. 22 (radio) Wil Tilroe-Otte/Shutterstock.com.

ISBN: 978-1-4777-2510-8
6-pack ISBN: 978-1-4777-2511-5

Manufactured in the United States of America

CPSIA Compliance Information: Batch #CS13RC: For further information contact Rosen Publishing, New York, New York at 1-800-237-9932.

Contents

An Inventor's Early Life

Nikola Tesla was a famous inventor who helped bring electricity to the world. He is also known as the inventor of radio. Nikola's discoveries are still used by people today!

Nikola was born in July of 1865. He grew up in a part of Europe that was called the Austro-Hungarian Empire. Now, we call it Croatia. Nikola's father was a **priest**, but his mother worked around the house. She invented things to make her housework easier. His mother's inventions opened Nikola's eyes to what he wanted to do when he grew up.

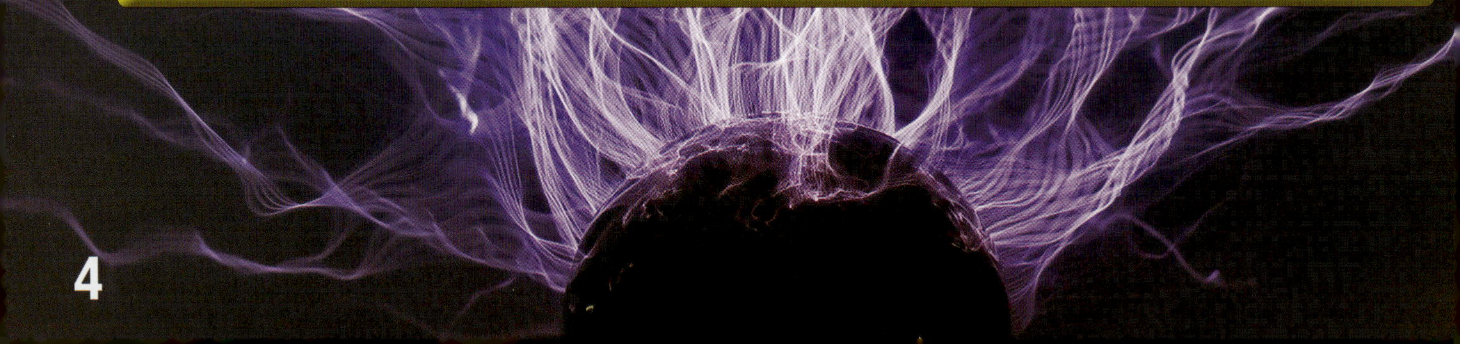

Nikola studied engineering in school.
Engineers use math and science to build things.

An Electric Idea!

While Nikola was in school, he came up with an idea for a new kind of **motor** that would change the world. It allowed the flow of energy in an electrical current to change directions. If the current could change directions, larger amounts of electricity could be sent over great distances to places like big cities. This new **technology** was called alternating current (AC) technology.

In order to work on his AC technology further, Nikola traveled to New York City in 1884. He wanted to work with Thomas Edison.

Thomas Edison

Thomas Edison was one of the most famous inventors of his time. Nikola thought Thomas would have an open mind about AC technology.

What's a Patent?

Nikola and Thomas didn't work together very long. They were very different people who didn't mix well together—like oil and water! Thomas didn't think that Nikola's AC technology was a good idea.

George Westinghouse, however, believed in Nikola's ideas. George bought the patent rights to all Nikola's AC technology in May of 1885. Patents are very important to inventors. They're rights, given by the government, to be the only person or company to make, use, and sell an invention for a certain number of years. George paid Nikola $60,000 for his patent rights.

George Westinghouse

George was a rich and powerful man. He was the head of the Westinghouse Electric Company in Pittsburgh, Pennsylvania.

From Chicago to New York

George and Nikola used AC technology to light one of the biggest events in the world at that time—the World's Fair! In 1893, the Chicago World's Fair was powered by AC technology, and it made Nikola famous.

That same year, Nikola was chosen to help build a power plant that used the energy of Niagara Falls to create electricity. This is called hydroelectric power. In 1896, the power plant began sending electricity to Buffalo, New York. It's still used today to send electricity to New York City.

Nikola dreamed for many years about using the power of Niagara Falls. With hard work, his dream came true!

No More Wires!

In addition to AC technology, Nikola worked his fingers to the bone trying to create wireless technology. It was his goal to someday be able to send energy from one place to another without using wires. In order to do this, he built a machine that took a household electrical current and sped it up to a much higher **frequency**. Nikola called the machine the Tesla coil. It was patented in 1891 and is still used in electronics, such as radios and televisions.

Tesla coils allow energy, such as electricity and sound, to be sent through the air from one place to another.

Nikola sent and received powerful radio **signals** using a Tesla coil. He showed his discovery to the public in New York City in 1898. Nikola created the first radio-controlled object—a boat that could move without wires. Nikola made the boat move using a small box that sent radio waves to it.

In 1899, Nikola traveled to Colorado Springs, Colorado, to work on other experiments. He created lightning for one of his experiments. This made the power go out throughout the whole city!

Nikola called his radio-controlled vehicle the first robot. We still use his technology to make toys like this one.

Who Invented Radio?

Nikola's patent for the invention of radio was granted in 1900. However, he soon had to fight over those rights with an Italian inventor, Guglielmo (gool-YEHL-moh) Marconi, who was working on his own radio experiments in England. Guglielmo's family had connections to rich people in England, which gave him a kind of power Nikola didn't have.

On December 12, 1901, Guglielmo sent the first radio signals across the Atlantic Ocean. Not even Nikola was able to do that! However, Nikola still held the American patent for radio, and Guglielmo used many of Nikola's inventions.

Guglielmo tried again and again to get a patent for radio in the United States, but the government turned him down for years.

After years of trying to get the government to give him a radio patent, Guglielmo finally succeeded in 1904. The U.S. Patent Office surprised everyone, especially Nikola, by changing its decision and giving Guglielmo a patent for radio.

In 1911, Guglielmo won the Nobel Prize—one of the most important prizes an inventor can win—for his work with radio. Nikola took steps to have his radio patent upheld. It took until a few months after his death in 1943 for it to happen.

Nikola didn't live to see the day when the U.S. Supreme Court—the highest court in America—upheld his patent for radio.

A Bright Inventor

Nikola kept working with electricity, radio, and other new inventions until the end of his life. His head was always full of ideas, but it was often hard for him to find money to make those ideas come to life. **Investors** sometimes felt his ideas were too big and it would be like throwing money away to try to carry them out.

Nikola died on January 7, 1943, in New York City. Today, he is remembered as one of the brightest inventors of his time.

Without Nikola, we wouldn't have many of the inventions we still use today!

One Man, Many Inventions

radio-controlled vehicles

Tesla coil

radio

AC technology

Glossary

frequency (FREE-kwuhn-see) The rate at which electricity keeps flowing in a current.

investor (ihn-VEHS-tuhr) A person who gives money to a person or a project that they think will make money in the future.

motor (MOH-tuhr) A machine that produces motion or power for doing work.

priest (PREEST) A person who leads or performs religious activities.

signal (SIHG-nuhl) A radio wave or electric current that sends a message or effect.

technology (tehk-NAH-luh-jee) A method that uses science to solve problems.

Index